AFTER

HAPPILY

EVER

AFTER

Rapunzel Lets Her Hair Down

First published in the United States in 2009
by Stone Arch Books
151 Good Counsel Drive, P.O. Box 669
Mankato, Minnesota 56002
www.stonearchbooks.com

First published by Orchard Books, a division of Hachette Children's Books.
338 Euston Road, London NW1 3BH, United Kingdom

Text copyright © Tony Bradman 2005
Illustrations copyright © Sarah Warburton 2005
The right of Tony Bradman to be identified as the author and Sarah
Warburton as the illustrator of this Work has been asserted by them in
accordance with the Copyright Designs and Patents Act 1988.

Library of Congress Cataloging-in-Publication Data
Bradman, Tony.
    [Rapunzel cuts loose]
    Rapunzel Lets Her Hair Down / by Tony Bradman; illustrated by
Sarah Warburton.
    p. cm. — (After Happily Ever After)
    Originally published: Rapunzel Cuts Loose. London: Orchard Books,
2005.
    ISBN 978-1-4342-1307-5 (library binding)
    [1. Sex role—Fiction. 2. Hair—Fiction.] I. Warburton, Sarah, ill.
II. Title.
PZ7.B7275Rap 2009
[Fic]—dc22   2008031836

Summary: Rapunzel is sick of living at the palace and sick of her long hair.
But the prince loves living in the palace and loves Rapunzel's long locks.
Find out if Rapunzel cuts her long hair and changes her life.

Creative Director: Heather Kindseth
Graphic Designer: Emily Harris

1 2 3 4 5 6 14 13 12 11 10 09

Printed in the United States of America

AFTER

HAPPILY EVER AFTER

Rapunzel Lets Her Hair Down

by Tony Bradman
illustrated by Sarah Warburton

STONE ARCH BOOKS
www.stonearchbooks.com

So Rapunzel and the Prince
lived happily ever after.
And then ...

It was Saturday, and Rapunzel and her husband, Prince Dynamo, were having breakfast at the palace. He was digging into his third bowl of royal cereal, but Rapunzel had barely touched her breakfast.

"Have you lost your appetite, my love?"
said Prince Dynamo. "What's wrong?"

"Oh, nothing much," said Rapunzel. She sighed. "I just don't like Saturdays, that's all."

"Really?" said Prince Dynamo, surprised. "What's not to like? I *love* Saturdays. I can spend the whole day doing the things I enjoy. It's golf this morning, tennis this afternoon, and a fencing match this evening."

"In case you've forgotten," said Rapunzel. "Saturday is the day that I wash my hair."

They both looked at the shining river of golden hair that flowed from Rapunzel's head, down her back, onto the floor, and around the table.

Twelve servants stood by to carry it, like the train of a dress.

Twelve more servants were needed to brush it, which usually took from breakfast until lunch.

And as for washing it, Rapunzel knew she'd be spending her Saturday in the royal bathroom.

Teams of servants would use enough water to float a ship and several huge barrels of shampoo.

Drying her hair would take until after midnight. The electric bills were enormous.

She hated the whole business, and so did the royal hairdresser.

He was always complaining that he never had anything interesting to do with her hair.

"I don't understand," said Prince Dynamo. "Is washing your hair a problem?"

"Well, yes," Rapunzel said nervously. "In fact, I've been thinking of getting my hair cut."

"You can't do that!" said Prince Dynamo, looking upset. "I love your long hair. It's what brought me to you in the first place!"

Rapunzel frowned. She'd had a
feeling this was going to be difficult.

Ever since Rapunzel had let down
her hair from a window, and the prince
had climbed up it to rescue her from the
wicked witch, he had talked about her
lovely, long locks.

"But it's a real pain," said Rapunzel.
"I'd love to play golf and tennis and
fence like you. I can't though, can I?"

"But I don't want you to change,"
said the prince. "I just want you to be
what you are now. Beautiful. Perfect.
With lovely, long hair. Besides, there's no
point in you taking up any sports. You'd
be terrible at them."

"Excuse me?" said a shocked Rapunzel.

"Oh, everybody knows girls are terrible at sports," Prince Dynamo said.

"I'm beginning to think the boys in the forest aren't too hot either. None of them are good enough to beat me. I can't seem to find anyone to play a decent game. Yikes, is that the time? Gotta go. Goodbye!"

The prince grabbed a piece of toast, blew her a kiss, and left. Rapunzel sat there scowling. So girls were bad at sports, were they? How dare he!

She had a good mind to summon the
royal hairdresser this instant and order
him to cut her hair off immediately. Then
she'd show the prince a thing or two!

That might not be such a great idea, she realized. The prince would probably make a fuss and want her to grow it back again. Besides, she really loved him, even if he was old fashioned. She just had to find a way to make them both happy.

In fact, what she needed was a plan. Rapunzel thought hard while her hair was being washed, but she didn't come up with anything.

After a while, she picked up a magazine and read an article about wigs. Now that's interesting, Rapunzel thought.

By Monday morning, Rapunzel had her plan. She waited until the prince left the palace for a game of tennis. Then she summoned the royal hairdresser.

"How may I serve you today, Your
Majesty?" he said, sounding bored already.
"Some advice on shampoo? A change of
hairbrush, perhaps?"

"Actually, I was thinking of asking you
to do something creative," said Rapunzel.

The Royal Hairdresser raised an
eyebrow. So Rapunzel took a deep breath
and told him her plan.

"Well, what do you think?" she said
when she'd finished. "Are you up for it?"

"You can definitely count me in," he
said, grinning. He pulled out his cell phone.
"I have some friends who'll be useful too."

And so began the transformation of Rapunzel. First, the royal hairdresser cut off her long hair.

"Are you absolutely sure?" he asked.

"Do it," said Rapunzel.

"It's cool, it's modern, it's just so you," said the royal hairdresser when he finished cutting.

Next, he and his team made a wig from the left over hair.

"It's a creative triumph," murmured the royal hairdresser, "even though I do say so myself!"

And finally, the royal hairdressing
team made her a very special costume.

But Rapunzel wasn't ready for the last part of her plan yet. She did lots of secret training first. She worked out at the gym.

She practiced all the prince's favorite sports. Nobody recognized her with her new hairstyle, of course.

She always made sure she was back
at the palace and wearing the wig
before the prince came home.

And soon she was ready. The moment
had come at last.

One morning, a few days later, Prince Dynamo was on the royal golf course with some friends, about to start a game. Suddenly, a strange masked figure jumped out from behind a bush and stood before him.

"Hold it right there, Prince Baby," growled the figure. "I am the Masked Mystery Girl, and I challenge you to a golf match. What do you say?"

"Play a girl?" said Prince Dynamo, laughing and looking around at his pals. "I don't think so. Now, would you mind?"

"Scared I'll beat you?" asked the Masked Mystery Girl.

"What!" sputtered Prince Dynamo. "All right, you're on. And I'll beat you hands down. FORE!"

But the Prince didn't beat the Masked
Mystery Girl. He didn't even get close.
She beat him easily.

The prince immediately challenged her to a game of something else, so they played tennis. She beat him at that too.

Then she beat him at bowling, badminton, fencing, horse racing, running, archery, swimming, and chess.

Then she beat him at darts and arm wrestling.

She even beat him at cards.

"That's it, I give up!" Prince Dynamo
groaned. He was exhausted and
bewildered as well. "I don't believe it.
Who are you?"

The Masked Mystery Girl smiled, then whipped off her mask.

"But . . ." sputtered the prince. "Rapunzel! Your hair! You look . . ." Rapunzel waited for him to finish, her heart beating fast. What if he hated it?

"You look absolutely fantastic!" he said. Prince Dynamo fell in love with Rapunzel all over again.

From that day on, they played lots of sports together. The Prince admitted he'd been wrong about girls and sports—especially since he still found it hard to beat Rapunzel.

And Rapunzel changed her hairstyle more often than the prince changed his socks, which meant the royal hairdresser had plenty to keep him busy.

So we can be sure that Rapunzel
and Prince Dynamo really did live
HAPPILY EVER AFTER!

THE END

ABOUT THE AUTHOR

Tony Bradman writes for children of all ages.
He is particularly well known for his top-selling
Dilly the Dinosaur series. His other titles include
the Happily Ever After series, The Orchard Book
of Heroes and Villains, and The Orchard Book of
Swords, Sorcerers, and Superheroes. Tony lives in
South East London.

ABOUT THE ILLUSTRATOR

Sarah Warburton is a rising star in children's
books. She is the illustrator of the Rumblewick
series, which has been very well received at an
international level. The series spans across both
picture books and fiction. She has also illustrated
nonfiction titles and the Happily Ever After series.
She lives in Bristol, England, with her young baby
and husband.

GLOSSARY

bewildered (bi-WIL-durd)—confused

rescue (RESS-kyoo)—to free someone from danger

scowling (SKOUL-ing)—frowning to show displeasure

servants (SUR-vuhnts)—people hired to perform household chores and personal errands

sputter (SPUHT-ur)—to speak with confusion or excitement

summon (SUHM-uhn)—to send for someone or something

train (TRANE)—the part of the dress that flows behind the person wearing it

transformation (transs-form-AY-shun)—in the process of being changed

triumph (TRYE-uhmf)—a great success

DISCUSSION QUESTIONS

1. Prince Dynamo didn't want Rapunzel to cut her hair. Why do you think change was so hard for him? What do you think would have happened if Rapunzel hadn't cut her hair?

2. When Rapunzel mentioned playing sports, Prince Dynamo laughed at her. However, girls didn't always get to play sports. How would you feel if girls still couldn't play sports?

3. In the end, Prince Dynamo and Rapunzel play lots of sports together. If you had to pick one team sport, what would it be and who would you play it with? Why?

WRITING PROMPTS

1. Pretend you are a hair dresser. How would you have convinced Rapunzel to change her look? Write a letter to Rapunzel and convince her to change her style.

2. When Rapunzel cuts her hair and puts on her costume, she becomes the Masked Mystery Girl. Her secret powers include great athletic ablility and cute hair. If you had to pick a mystery name, what would it be? Write a description of your new name and your secret powers.

3. It takes an entire day to wash Rapunzel's hair, and it's a chore that she hates! Make a list of at least ten excuses that Rapunzel could use to get out of washing her hair.

Before there was **HAPPILY EVER AFTER**,
there was **ONCE UPON A TIME** ...

GRAPHIC SPIN

Read the **ORIGINAL** fairy tales in **NEW** graphic novel retellings.

INTERNET SITES

Do you want to know more about subjects related to this book? Or are you interested in learning about other topics? Then check out FactHound, a fun, easy way to find Internet sites.

Our investigative staff has already sniffed out great sites for you!

Here's how to use FactHound:

1. Visit *www.facthound.com*

2. Select your grade level.

3. To learn more about subjects related to this book, type in the book's ISBN number: **1434213072**.

4. Click the **Fetch It** button.

FactHound will fetch the best Internet sites for you!